THE POWER OF
Gandhi

L. L. OWENS

STECK-VAUGHN
Harcourt Supplemental Publishers

www.steck-vaughn.com

Photography: Cover ©Vithalbhai/Dinodia Picture Agency/Sipa Press; p.iv ©Bettmann/CORBIS; p.4 ©Vithalbhai/Dinodia Picture Agency/Sipa Press; p.6 ©Associated Press/AP/Wide World; p.8 ©Associated Press/AP/Wide World; p.10 ©Arthur Schatz/TimePix; p.13 ©Hulton Archive/Getty Images; p.14 ©Margaret Bourke-White/TimePix; p.17a ©Hulton Archive/Getty Images; p.17b ©Vithalbhai/Dinodia Picture Agency/Sipa Press; p.19 ©Vithalbhai/Dinodia Picture Agency/Sipa Press; p.20 ©Henri Cartier-Bresson/Magnum Photos; p.22 ©Bettmann/CORBIS; p.23 Courtesy of GandhiServe Foundation.

ISBN 0-7398-7512-4

Copyright © 2004 Steck-Vaughn, a division of Harcourt Supplemental Publishers, Inc. All rights reserved. No part of the material protected by this copyright may be reproduced or utilized in any form or by any means, electronic or mechanical, including photocopying, recording, or by any information storage and retrieval system, without permission in writing from the copyright owner. Requests for permission to make copies of any part of the work should be mailed to: Copyright Permissions, Steck-Vaughn, P.O. Box 26015, Austin, Texas 78755.

Power Up! Building Reading Strength is a trademark of Steck-Vaughn.

Printed in China.

2 3 4 5 6 7 8 9 M 07

Contents

Introduction
Setting the Scene 1

Chapter 1
Gandhi's Early Years 2

Chapter 2
Gandhi Starts His Life's Journey 7

Chapter 3
Life in South Africa 11

Chapter 4
Gandhi Leads the Way 13

Chapter 5
The End of Gandhi's Journey 18

Glossary 24

Index 28

The British Empire 1869

Areas of British Rule

- Arctic Ocean
- Great Britain
- Europe
- Asia
- Mediterranean Sea
- Gambia
- Sierra Leone
- Gold Coast
- Africa
- Arabian Sea
- India
- Bay of Bengal
- Atlantic Ocean
- Cape Colony (South Africa)
- Indian Ocean

Introduction

Setting the Scene

A boy who would change the world was born in India in 1869. The boy's name was Mohandas Gandhi.

The British Empire **ruled** India then. It had ruled parts of India for about 200 years.

The Indian people had to follow British **laws.** Many Indian people thought the laws were not fair. They wanted change.

Gandhi became an important leader who helped free India from British rule. He also worked to end **prejudice.** What Gandhi did during his life was only the beginning of his power, though. Gandhi's life changed the lives of many.

Chapter 1

Gandhi's Early Years

Gandhi's father was a city **leader.** He was one of the most important men in town. Gandhi learned to tell the truth from his father.

Gandhi was close to his mother. He learned about his family's **religion** from her. Gandhi's family practiced Hinduism.

Gandhi's family had more money than many people in India had. They were in one of the higher **castes,** or classes of people.

Hindu Castes

Hindu people were **ranked** by their jobs. Gandhi's family was in the Vaisya caste.

The poorest people in India were known as Untouchables. They were ranked low and were **treated** badly.

A Hindu who touched an Untouchable would **pray** that nothing bad had rubbed off from that person. Then the Hindu would clean his or her body.

Gandhi never believed in this Hindu practice. Later in his life he helped the Untouchables. He hated to see them **suffer.** He called them "children of God."

Hindu Classes

Brahman (BRAH muhn)
wise ones, teachers

Kshatriya (kuh SHAT ree yuh)
guards, rulers

Vaisya (VYS yuh)
farmers, artists, sales people, city leaders

Sudra (SOO druh)
workers

....

Untouchable
bathroom and street cleaners

School Days

Gandhi was going to school by age seven. He took classes in languages, math, and geography.

Once, a teacher saw that Gandhi was writing a wrong answer on a spelling test. The teacher was angry. He told Gandhi to copy the right answer from another boy. Gandhi wouldn't do it. He believed in doing his own work.

Gandhi was smaller than most boys his age. He did not like **sports** and he had big ears. Gandhi was afraid that other boys would make fun of him. As he got older, though, Gandhi had lots of friends. He liked to spin tops and play games with them.

Gandhi is shown here at age seven.

An Important Lesson

Few people today can picture Gandhi getting into trouble. Like other children, though, Gandhi was not perfect.

Sometimes he ate meat with his friends. Eating meat was against his religion.

Once he took money from his family. He used it to buy things for himself. Gandhi felt bad. He knew that taking money was wrong. He wanted to tell the truth, so he wrote a letter to his father to tell him what he had done.

Gandhi's father didn't say a word. He did not hit Gandhi. He just cried and ripped up the letter. By not hitting his son while angry, Gandhi's father was practicing **nonviolence.**

Gandhi later said that he had learned a lot about **forgiveness** that day. Gandhi would remember this lesson and teach it to others for the rest of his life.

Young Gandhi Marries

When Gandhi was just 13 years old, he got married. The girl's name was Kasturba. She was the same age as Gandhi. His mother and father had picked Kasturba to be Gandhi's wife six years earlier.

The two didn't like being married at first. They had many fights. They got to know each other, though, and they later fell in love. Kasturba helped Gandhi with his important work. The two were married for 62 years.

Gandhi and Kasturba married in 1882.

Chapter 2

Gandhi Starts His Life's Journey

First Stop: Law School

Gandhi started his life's biggest **journey** by going to law school in London, England. He was 19. He missed Kasturba and their new baby boy. He missed his mother, too. Gandhi's father had died a few years before.

In London, Gandhi found a place to live. He bought new suits, a silver-topped walking stick, and a top hat. He took lessons in French, music, and dancing.

Gandhi then decided to spend more time on his law classes. He did well.

Gandhi (center) sits with friends in front of his law office.

Gandhi's Favorite Books

Gandhi read as much as he could. Later in his life, Gandhi joked that the time he spent in **jail** helped him catch up on his reading. He loved these books:

Bhagavad-Gita
Holy Bible
Koran
The Kingdom of God Is Within You
    by Leo Tolstoy
On the Duty of Civil Disobedience
    by Henry David Thoreau
Unto This Last by John Ruskin

After law school Gandhi moved back to India. He learned that his mother had died.

Jobs were hard to find in India. In 1893 Gandhi took a job in South Africa. There, his long journey to end prejudice began.

A Life-Changing Train Ride

One day Gandhi was on a train. A white man was upset to see Gandhi there. He wanted the Indian to leave. This was **racism.**

Gandhi said that he had **paid** his money and had the right to be there. He wouldn't move. A guard threw him off the train.

This was one of the first times Gandhi was hurt by racism. It made him think. He asked:
- What do I believe in?
- How should I live my life?

Gandhi believed that all people should **accept** each other and live together in **peace.** He believed in love and forgiveness. He wanted to share these truths with others.

Gandhi decided that his life would be an **example.** He said, "My life is my message."

Truth Force

Gandhi worked hard to win the same rights for all people. He followed the Hindu idea of **satyagraha.** This is also called "truth force." It means standing up for what is right. It also means that doing so must never lead to **violence.**

When Gandhi was on the train, he did not get angry. He just said what he knew was true: He had every right to his seat.

Gandhi did not fight with the guard then, but he did not move on his own, either. What Gandhi did on the train is called **nonviolent noncooperation.**

Gandhi used what he had learned in law school to help Indians win the right to sit in the train seats they paid for.

Cesar Chavez used satyagraha in his fight for the rights of farm workers.

Chapter 3

Life in South Africa

Like India, in 1893 the country of South Africa was under British rule. Gandhi saw that Indians in South Africa were not treated fairly. He spent the next twenty years trying to make life better for Indians in South Africa.

He talked to people about nonviolent noncooperation. He started many **protests.** He wrote letters to leaders and spoke to large gatherings of people.

Sometimes Gandhi **fasted,** or stopped eating. He did not pay **taxes** that he thought were not fair. Many times Gandhi was thrown in jail for his acts.

Making News

Gandhi had many **followers** in South Africa. He led the Natal Indian Congress. This **group** of people worked for Indians' rights in a part of South Africa called Natal.

Newspapers wrote about Gandhi. The world learned how the British were treating people of color.

In 1899 the Boer War started in South Africa. The British and the Dutch were fighting about land. Gandhi helped the British because he was Indian and the British ruled India.

Afterwards, Gandhi kept fighting racism in South Africa. He and his followers always used nonviolent ways.

By 1915 Gandhi had helped Indians living in South Africa win better rights. Gandhi felt that his work in South Africa was done. Gandhi was ready to take *satyagraha* to India. He was ready to go home.

Chapter 4

Gandhi Leads the Way

The Great Soul Spreads His Message

When Gandhi returned to India in 1915, he traveled all over the country to speak of peace, love, and nonviolence.

Gandhi was known and well-loved by the people in India. Some Indian people called him *Bapu.* That means "father of the country." Most people called him *Mahatma,* which means "Great Soul."

Gandhi felt that the British should leave India. He told Indians why he thought the British should leave. The British did not want to leave, and they did not want to change the laws.

Gandhi spoke often to explain why the British should leave India.

Whenever Gandhi was **arrested,** people all over the world knew it. They read about his time in jail in the newspapers. They watched and waited as he fasted. He was willing to suffer for his **beliefs.**

Gandhi had long since given away most of his things. He had started some farming towns, or **ashrams.** There, people built their own homes, made their own clothing, and grew their own food. Anyone was welcome to join. The castes did not matter in an *ashram.*

Gandhi lived in a small house in one of his *ashrams.* He could often be found working at his spinning wheel. He dressed in a plain, white cloth. This was how people in the lower castes dressed.

Kasturba lived as Gandhi did. She and Gandhi passed on their beliefs and way of life to their four sons. Harilal was the oldest son, born in 1887. He was followed by brothers Manilal in 1891, Ramdas in 1896, and Devadas in 1899.

The Salt March

In 1930, Gandhi started one of his biggest protests ever—the Salt March. Indians had to pay a high tax when they bought salt. People needed salt, and the British knew that Indians would have to buy it and pay the tax.

This high tax was not fair, and Gandhi wouldn't stand for it. He began walking 240 miles to the sea. He was going to gather salt that had been left on the sand by the salty waves of the sea. Thousands of people joined him as he walked. The trip took 24 days.

◀ **Gandhi often read or worked at his spinning wheel.**

At the sea Gandhi picked up a bit of salt. He held it up for everyone to see. Then he turned around and started the long walk home. His followers did the same.

This act showed the British that Indians would not buy salt from the British. They would not pay the tax, either.

After the march about 60,000 Indians were arrested for making their own salt from the sea. Gandhi was arrested as well.

The British understood that times had changed. Maybe it was time to think about letting India rule itself. In 1931 they asked Gandhi to come to London to talk about it. This was a start, but it would be another 16 years before India was free.

Using *Satyagraha*

In jail again in 1932, Gandhi fasted for six days. He became **weaker** with each passing day.

The world was watching Gandhi, and the British were afraid. What if he died? The British didn't want to be **blamed** for that.

Thousands of Indians joined Gandhi on the Salt March. He picked up salt from the beach instead of paying the British tax.

The British said that they would give rights to the Untouchables if Gandhi would end his fast. Gandhi agreed, and he was freed from jail. Gandhi had won by using *satyagraha*.

Gandhi said that helping India was easy. He said that all he had done was tell the British that they could not tell him what to do in his own country.

Chapter 5

The End of Gandhi's Journey

By 1942 many Indians felt that the time had come to make the British leave India. They held nonviolent protests. They were ready to die for their beliefs.

Soon, though, violence broke out across the country. Gandhi was blamed and thrown in jail. Kasturba was arrested a few days later. She was sent to jail with Gandhi.

In 1944 Kasturba got sick while she was in jail. She died there, in Gandhi's arms. Gandhi was freed about six weeks later.

India Is Free But Not at Peace

On August 15, 1947, the British leaders left India. At last India would rule itself. It had been a long, hard journey for Gandhi and his followers.

Lord and Lady Mountbatten stand with Gandhi. Lord Mountbatten was the last British leader of India.

Instead of becoming one country, though, India was cut in two. One side became India, which was Hindu. The other side became Pakistan, which was Muslim. The people who lived on the two sides had different religions. Fighting broke out between Hindus and Muslims, and about 500,000 people were killed.

Gandhi was sad and angry. He asked the two sides to come together as brothers and sisters. He said they could **forgive** each other.

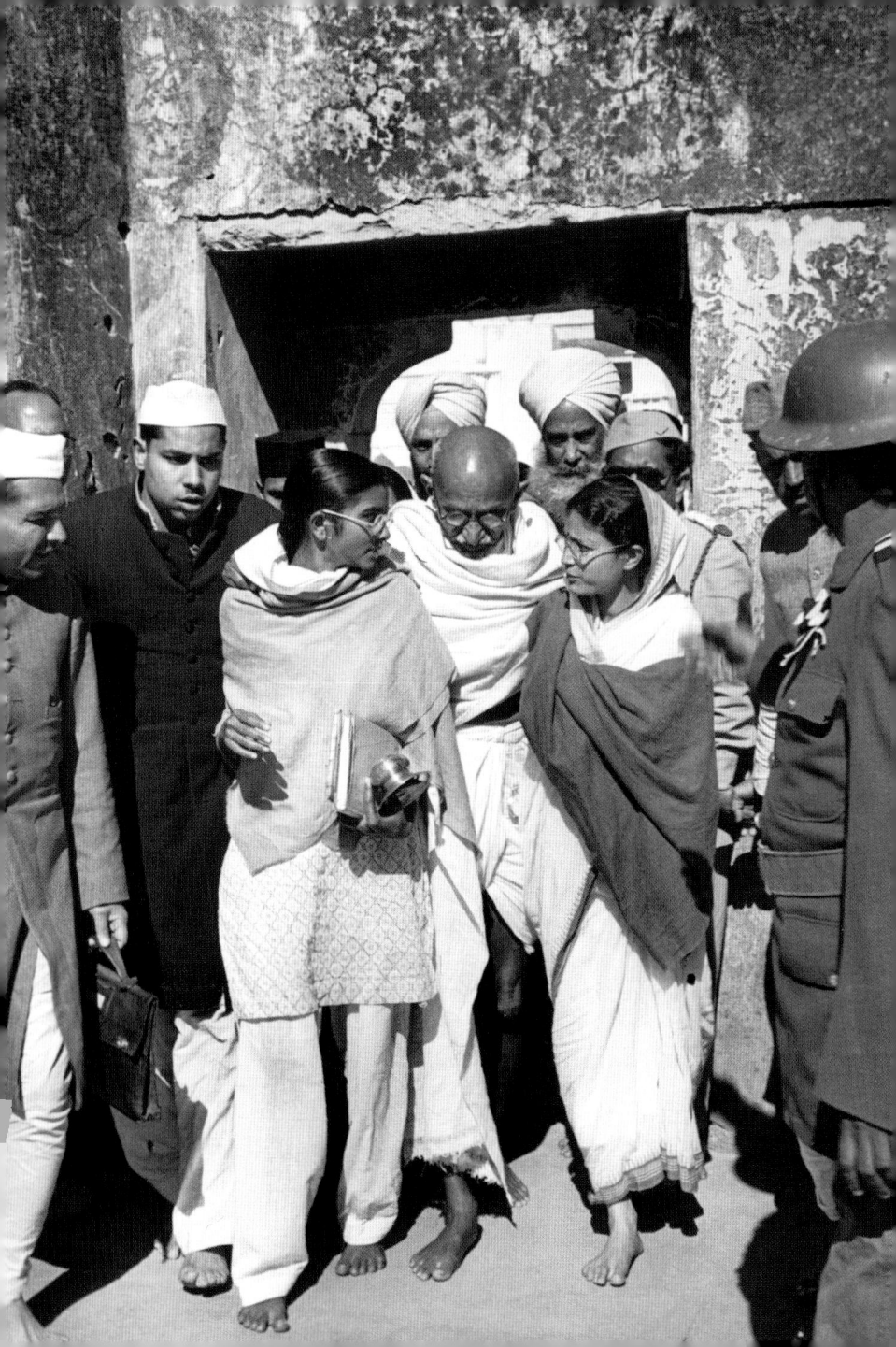

Gandhi's Last Days

Six months later, Hindus and Muslims were still fighting. Gandhi went to visit the cities of Calcutta and Delhi. He fasted and asked for peace. People stopped fighting, and they agreed to listen to Gandhi.

Gandhi gathered about 500 people together on January 30, 1948, to pray for peace. The 78-year-old Gandhi was thin and weak from fasting. He needed help walking. People bowed as Gandhi passed.

A man named Nathuram Godse pushed to the front of the group. He bowed in front of Gandhi. As Gandhi prayed, Godse shot Gandhi three times.

Gandhi fell to the ground. He forgave Godse. He said, "Hai Rama, hai Rama." That meant "Oh God, oh God."

Those were Gandhi's last words.

◀ **Gandhi walks to his final gathering.**

Gandhi Lives On

The people of the world were sad to lose Gandhi. They remember him, even today.

Gandhi's life was a great example to others.
- He helped Indians win their rights.
- He showed people how to join together to face problems without violence.
- He showed people how to stand up for their beliefs.
- He showed people how to love, accept, and forgive one another.

People in many countries have followed Gandhi's teachings and used them to change lives. Gandhi's mark on the world will last forever.

These are the only things that Gandhi owned when he died:
- 1 desk set
- 1 pair of eyeglasses
- 1 pocket watch
- 1 tin bowl
- 1 cloth
- 2 spoons
- 2 pots
- 2 pairs of sandals
- 3 books
- 3 small toy monkeys

Glossary

accept (ak SEHPT) *verb* To accept is to agree with or to like someone or something.

arrested (uh REHST ihd) *adjective* Arrested means taken away by the police.

ashrams (AHSH ruhmz) *noun* Ashrams are places where people live and make everything they need.

beliefs (buh LEEFS) *noun* Beliefs are ideas that people feel they know are true.

blamed (BLAYMD) *adjective* To be blamed means to be believed to have started a problem.

castes (KASTS) *noun* Castes are classes of people that Hindus were born into.

example (eg ZAM puhl) *noun* An example is an act or thing that shows how to do something.

fasted (FAST ihd) *verb* Fasted means did not eat anything.

followers (FAHL oh uhrz) *noun* Followers are people who do as the lead person does.

forgive (fuhr GIHV) *verb* To forgive someone means to stop being angry about something that person did.

forgiveness (fuhr GIHV nihs) *noun* Forgiveness is the act of not being angry about something that a person did or said.

group (GROOP) *noun* A group is two or more things or people.

guards (GAHRDZ) *noun* Guards are people who watch over places, people, or things.

jail (JAYL) *noun* Jail is a place where people are held by the police.

journey (JUR nee) *noun* A journey is a trip from one place to another.

laws (LAWZ) *noun* Laws tell people what they can and cannot do.

leader (LEED uhr) *noun* A leader is a person who does something first. Other people do as the leader does.

nonviolence (nahn VY uh luhns) *noun* Nonviolence is the act of not hurting anyone.

nonviolent noncooperation (nahn VY uh luhnt nahn koh ahp uhr AY shuhn) *noun* Nonviolent noncooperation means not hurting anyone while not doing what someone wants you to do.

paid (PAYD) *verb* Paid means gave money for something.

peace (PEES) *noun* Peace is time without fighting.

pray (PRAY) *verb* To pray is to talk to something or someone you believe to be greater than all people.

prejudice (PREHJ uh dihs) *noun* Prejudice is deciding what you think about people before you know them.

protests (PROH tehsts) *noun* Protests are acts that show that one does not agree with something.

racism (RAY sihz uhm) *noun* Racism is being mean to people because of their skin color.

ranked (RANGKD) *adjective* Ranked means put in an order.

religion (rih LIHJ uhn) *noun* Religion is the practice of what one believes.

ruled (ROOLD) *verb* Ruled means was in charge of something.

satyagraha (SUHT yuh gruh huh) *noun* Satyagraha is a Hindu word that means "truth force."

sports (SPAWRTS) *noun* Sports are games that people play together.

suffer (SUHF uhr) *verb* To suffer means to put up with hard times.

taxes (TAKS ihz) *noun* Taxes are money that one must pay to one's country.

treated (TREET ihd) *adjective* Treated means someone has acted toward you in a certain way.

violence (VY uh luhnts) *noun* Violence is the act of hurting someone by hitting, kicking, shooting, and so on.

weaker (WEEK uhr) *adjective* Weaker means not as strong.

Index

ashrams 14
Boer War 12
Brahman 3
British Empire 1
Calcutta, India 21
castes 2–3, 14
Delhi, India 21
forgiveness 5, 9, 19, 22
Godse, Nathuram 21
Hindu, Hinduism 2–3, 10, 19, 21
India 1, 9, 11–13, 17–19, 21
Kasturba 6–7, 15, 18
Kshatriya 3
London, England 7, 16
Mountbatten, Lord and Lady 19
Natal Indian Congress 12
nonviolence 5, 10–12, 22
nonviolent noncooperation 10–11
Pakistan 19
peace 9, 21
prejudice 1, 9
protests 11, 15–16, 18
racism 9, 12
Salt March 15–17
satyagraha 10, 12, 16–17
South Africa 9–12
Untouchables 2–3, 17
Vaisya 2–3
violence 10, 22